For my daughter, Lily, and
for everyone who has ever
wondered if they belong ...
Trust me — you do.

ISBN: 978-1-913339-35-7
Text copyright – Annette Demetriou 2022
Illustrations copyright – Angela Mayers 2022

Me, in the Middle

Written by Annette Demetriou
Illustrated by Angela Mayers

First published in the UK
March 2022 by Owlet Press
www.owletpress.com

It was a sunny afternoon, and stretched out across the playground like a colourful, patchwork quilt was A HUGE MAP!

Miss Clark only let us chalk pictures THIS big for SPECIAL lessons ...

"OK, everyone, I want you to find the country where WE live!" said Miss Clark, smiling. There was a scuffle as we all tried to make it onto England. One toe would have to do, I thought, clinging to Seren's hand to stop her falling into the sea!

Miss Clark beamed. "I can see you've ALL done your homework. Great job! Today we're going to be learning more about families."

Miss Clark explained that family trees show different generations in a family, all connected like branches. "Who knows – some of you could be related to royalty!" she laughed. Everyone gasped, hoping to be cousins with a duchess.

"And we can add all sorts of information to our family tree to make it beautiful, just like this map. Let's try something else – everyone hop over to the country that your parents come from."

There was another scuffle
as everyone noisily rushed
around the map again.

This time, I stayed still.

"Which parent?" I whispered to Seren, as she let go of my hand and planted herself firmly in Wales.

"I don't know!" she mouthed.

I dithered in the Atlantic Ocean, getting more and more confused.

"5!" shouted Miss Clark. "4, 3 ..."

"Georgie's in the sea-aa! Blooop bloop blorrrrp!" gurgled tell-tale Ben.

"She's a magical mermaid!" said Seren, sticking her tongue out at Ben.

I panicked and ran back towards England, but there was no room for me there, so I circled down towards Africa.

"2 ... and ...1!"

"Georgie, have you found the right country?" Miss Clark asked. I quickly leapt over to East Africa, but then Ben kept shouting, "Why are YOU in Africa?"

"How wonderful to see that our families come from all over the world," said Miss Clark, above the hum of voices. "Akari, you found Japan ALL on your own! Arjun well done for showing us the exact region of India your parents come from. Luca – loving your carnival dance moves over in Brazil."

As Miss Clark got to me, people started giggling, so I jumped back into the sea!

Everyone was staring at ME ... in the middle.

"What ARE you doing, Georgie? Could you hop over to join the others please?" she asked, pointing towards England.

But no one would make room for me. "Go back to East Africa," shouted Dan the Destroyer.

"She's too pale! You have to have brown skin if your mum and dad are from a hot country," said Effia, frowning.

Just then, the bell rang. My tummy ached and my heart felt heavy. Maybe I didn't belong ... anywhere?

I really didn't want to work on my family tree over the weekend ...
I knew it would show how different I was feeling ...
stuck out on a lonely branch, on my own.

But Mum and Dad thought it would help to stick photos
on my tree, so we could see the whole family.

And when we finished ...
it turned out to be beautiful.

Full of colour and so
wide, that it stretched
all the way across
the Atlantic Ocean,
from England ...
to East Africa!

With ME
in the middle!

"The higher it goes, the more countries it touches."
I explained the next day in class.

"It goes to Spain, across to
Portugal and even up to Scotland!"

"My mum's family have light skin, with pretty freckles,

and Dad's family, from Uganda, are brown and beautiful, with rich dark hair that has coily curls."

Miss Clark nodded proudly. "I'm SO impressed with the effort you've put into your family tree, Georgie!"

She gave me a shiny gold sticker for excellent work!

"This shows us why we should NEVER judge someone by their
skin, or colour of their hair, or shape of their features.
We are SO MUCH MORE than what can be seen at first glance."

The next day, as a treat, we had a picnic of 'family dishes' to share in the park.

Miss Clark said it was another way to add even more information to our family trees. This time it felt good being in the middle of something this wonderful.

Then we went to look at the different
trees in the park, to see how they
compared to our own family trees.

The weeping willows stretched out wide,
with green and gold leaves mixed together,
a bit like MY family tree.

The fig trees were wide, but very short, a
bit like Ben's family tree, which stopped
suddenly, as no one really knew who
came above his grandparents.

Glittering in the sunshine was a sweet wild plum tree. Its trunk had grown apart and then formed two new, healthier trunks. "This is just like mine," said Kiki, whose parents were separated.

Akari's was tall and narrow like the pine trees: her family tree went back forever, but each branch was small.

"I'm an only child, which means I don't have any brothers or sisters. But that's okay — Mum, Grandad AND Great Grandma are just like me!" she told us.

I thought Seren's was the best. Her family tree was twisty-turny and strong like a big oak. It went one way, for her birth parents, and then another way for her adoptive mums, before booming up wide and tall, like mine.

"Don't you mind?" I asked Seren.
She shook her head, grinning.

"My mums CHOSE me. It feels really
special to get TWO trees stuck together!"

It was actually really exciting to see how
special it was to be different. But in many
ways, we are also the same ...

"All of these trees are beautiful." said Miss Clark. "So many different colours and shapes, like our family trees.

All their roots dig down into the same rich earth ..."

I smiled proudly.
"Yes! And we are
right in the middle!"

Make your own family tree!